ZOMO
The Rabbit

A TRICKSTER TALE FROM WEST AFRICA

TOLD AND ILLUSTRATED BY
Gerald McDermott

Voyager Books • Harcourt, Inc.

San Diego   New York   London

For information about permission to reproduce selections from this book,
please write to Permissions, Houghton Mifflin Harcourt Publishing
Company 215 Park Avenue South NY NY 10003.

First Voyager Books edition 1996
Voyager Books is a trademark of Harcourt, Inc., registered in the
United States of America and/or other jurisdictions.

The Library of Congress has cataloged the hardcover edition as follows:
McDermott, Gerald.
Zomo the rabbit: a trickster tale from West Africa/told and illustrated by
Gerald McDermott.
p. cm.
Summary: Zomo the rabbit, an African trickster, sets out to gain wisdom.
[1. Folklore—Africa, West.]   I. Title.
PZ8.1.M159Zo   1992
398.2—dc20   91-14558
[E]
ISBN 0-15-299967-1
ISBN 0-15-201010-6 pb

SCP 28 27 26 25 24 23
4500491250

Printed in China

The paintings in this book were done in gouache on heavyweight
hot-press watercolor paper.
Color separations by Bright Arts, Ltd., Singapore
Printed and bound by RR Donnelley, China
Production supervision by Warren Wallerstein and Diana Ford
Designed by Lydia D'moch

Zomo the Rabbit is a prominent member of the
family of animal tricksters that populate the
traditional tales of West Africa. These humorous
stories of mischief and cunning are told to
instruct as well as to entertain and have been
kept alive by the powerful oral traditions of the
African peoples.

There are many links between these African
tales and their cultural descendants in the New
World. Zomo, though separated from his origins
in Hausaland, Nigeria, by an ocean and several
centuries, lives on as Cunny Rabbit or Compere
Lapin in the Caribbean and as Brer Rabbit in the
United States.

Like tricksters in storytelling traditions around
the world, the fleet-footed Zomo outwits his
larger foes with guile and trickery. And like his
African cousins Spider and Tortoise, he uses his
wit to gain wisdom.

—G.M.

For Jimena

Zomo!

Zomo the rabbit.
He is not big.
He is not strong.
But he is very clever.

Time was, Zomo wanted *more* than cleverness — he wanted wisdom! He went to Sky God and asked for it.

"Zomo, it is not so simple," said Sky God.
"To get wisdom, you must earn it."

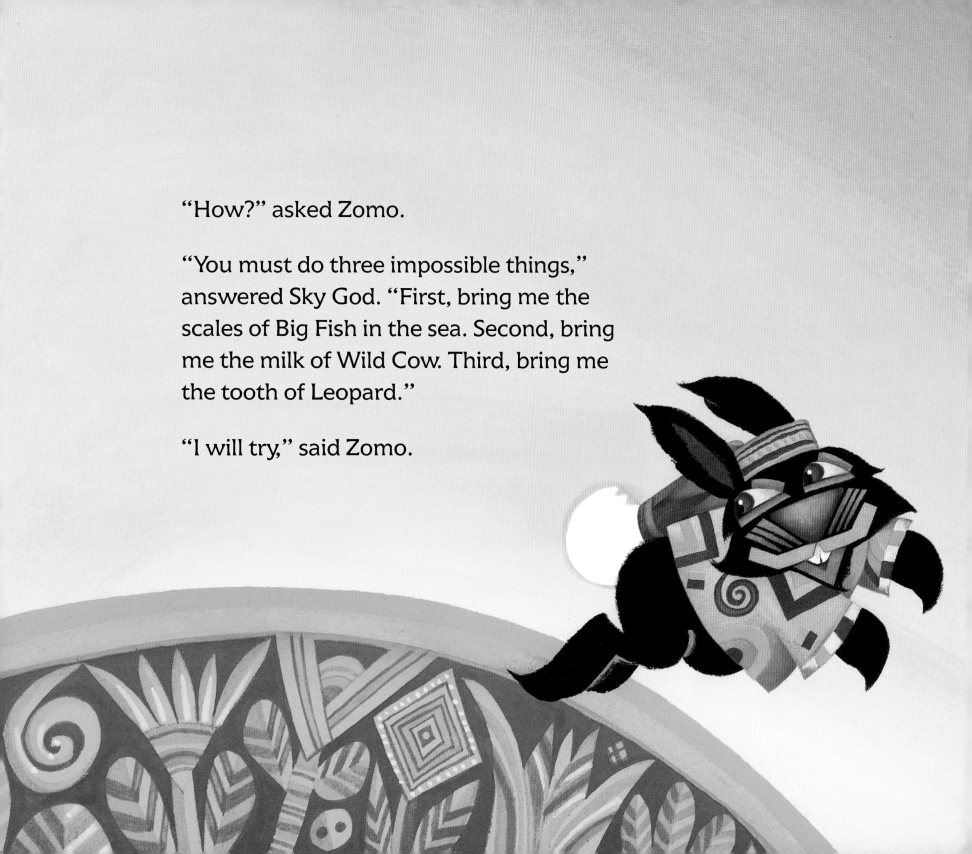

"How?" asked Zomo.

"You must do three impossible things," answered Sky God. "First, bring me the scales of Big Fish in the sea. Second, bring me the milk of Wild Cow. Third, bring me the tooth of Leopard."

"I will try," said Zomo.

Zomo went to the edge of the sea.
He began to play his drum.
He played so loud his drumbeats went
down to the bottom of the sea.

Deep below, Big Fish heard the music of
the drum.

Big Fish came up out of the water.
He danced on the sand.

Faster and faster, Zomo beat his drum.
Faster and faster, Big Fish danced.

Big Fish danced so fast his scales fell off.

Big Fish was naked.

Splash! He jumped back into the sea.

Quickly, Zomo scooped up the fish scales
in his hat and hopped into the forest.

In the forest, Zomo climbed a palm tree.
He looked all around.
Then he saw Wild Cow.

"Ha!" laughed Zomo.
"You are not so big!
You are not strong!"

"Who is that laughing at me?" asked Wild Cow.

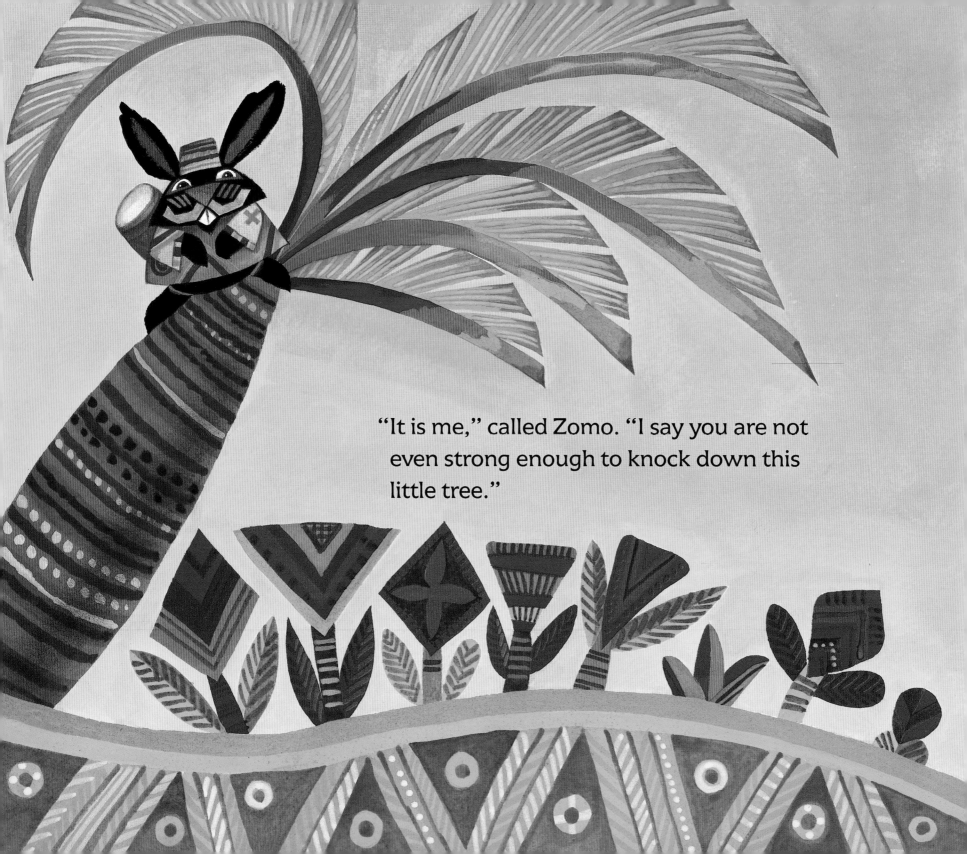

"It is me," called Zomo. "I say you are not even strong enough to knock down this little tree."

Wild Cow got angry.
She ran at the tree to knock it down.

Thump! She hit that tree.
But the palm tree was soft.
Her horns got stuck.

Quickly, Zomo slid down
the tree.

He turned his drum upside down and filled it with milk.

By the time Wild Cow got unstuck, Zomo was far away.

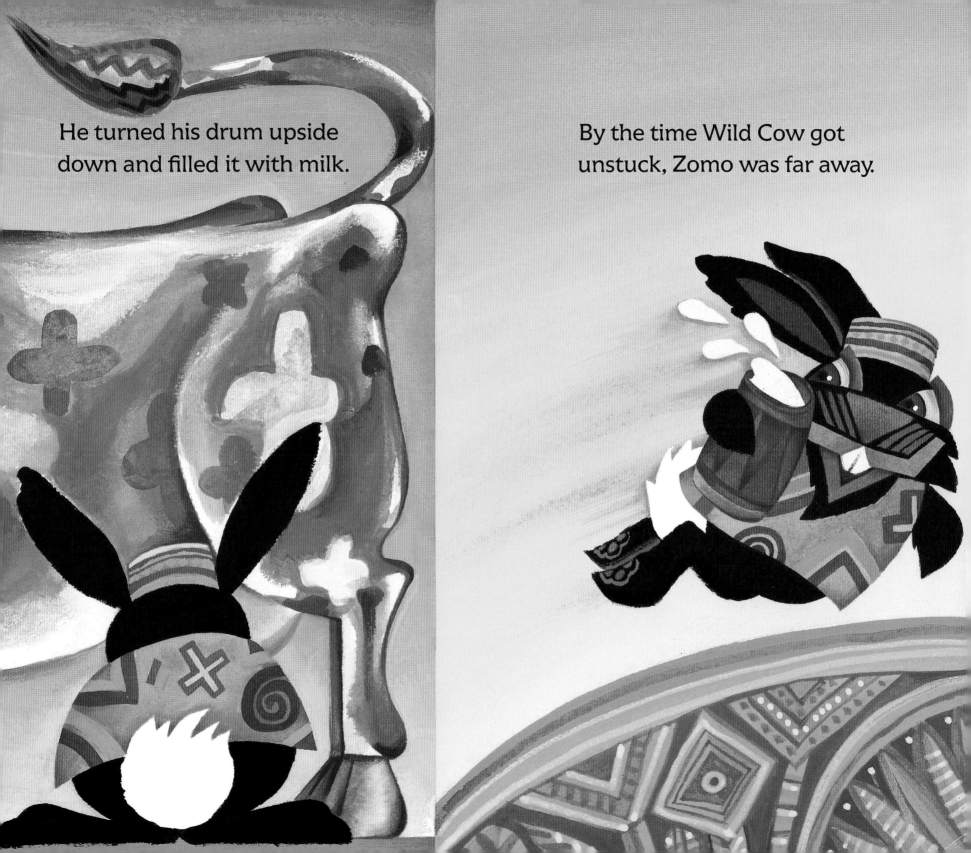

Zomo took the path to the top of
a high hill.
It was the hill where Leopard
walked every day.
Zomo tipped his hat and sprinkled
a few fish scales on the path.

Zomo tipped his drum and spilled
a few drops of milk on the path.

Then Zomo went to the bottom of the hill.
He hid behind a rock.

Soon Leopard came walking over the hill.
He slipped on the slippery scales and
the milk.

He rolled down the hill.

Bump! Leopard hit the rock.
His tooth popped out.

Up jumped Zomo.
He caught that tooth.
Quickly, he hopped away.

Zomo took the scales of Big Fish,
the milk of Wild Cow,
and the tooth of Leopard to Sky God.

Sky God smiled upon Zomo.
"You are clever enough to do
the impossible," he said.
"Now I will give you wisdom."

Sky God spoke.
Zomo listened.

"Three things in this world are worth having: courage, good sense, and caution," said Sky God. "Little rabbit, you have lots of courage, a bit of sense, but no caution. So next time you see Big Fish, or Wild Cow, or Leopard . . .

". . . better run fast!"

Zomo is not big.
Zomo is not strong.
But now Zomo has wisdom.
And he is very, very fast.